all the rot

j. daniel west

remember, no one is alone on their journey.

First published in Great Britain by Written Off Publishing, 2025
Copyright © J. Daniel West, 2025
The moral right of the author has been asserted.

All rights reserved. No part of this book may be reproduced in any form or by any electronic or mechanical means, including information storage and retrieval systems, without permission in writing from the publisher, except by reviewers, who may quote brief passages in a review.

Written Off does not use AI.

ISBN: 978-1-915320-47-6

Written Off Publishing
Owley Wood Road
Weaverham
Cheshire
CW8 3LF

writtenoffpublishing.com

Edited by Rebecca Kenny @ Written Off
Cover art © Sekinue, @sekinue

Printed in the UK on recycled paper using sustainable inks by Mixam Ltd.

*For everyone who's been on this journey
and those still travelling it*

contents

dirt

the sleeping man	13
wait	14
burst ventricle, broken heart	16
with every bite of every fruit	18
energy cannot be destroyed, only changed	19
three flies on the severed head of a mouse	20
if i gave you an orchard, you'd go mad	22
horoscope funeral	24
small	25
winter sun	26
the cruel face of lazarus	28
the stranger in my grandad's coffin	29
ebb...	30
legacy	32
measuring catastrophic events	33
do you hear that memory?	34
a table set for four	36
trade network	37
ocean moth	38
i have no body	40
ship of theseus	42
sleeping lessons	43
obsessions with black hole theories	44
fan belt	47
limits	48
visitation at the infinite prison	50
unrequited	52
cassandra	53
i used to like museums but now i'm not so sure	54
divergence and fault	56
a second earthquake would have been less memorable	58
helicopter	60
broken things make for gorgeous sculptures	61

decomposition
    finding the gate that takes me home — 65
    superstitious limbs — 66
    peculiar behaviour — 67
    a place to sit — 68
    something to crush in the rain — 70
    nesting time — 71
    waste as medicine — 72
    still — 73
    little lobster boy — 74
    water off a duck's back — 78
    hometown magnification — 80
    an odd number of cycles — 82
    i think we're lost — 84
    confession — 85
    in which i am both orpheus and eurydice — 86
    return fire — 87
    dew, inhabited — 88
    trying to make being good an unconscious bodily process — 89
    wikipedia page funeral — 90
    a palmful is a body of water — 92
    diametrically opposed clocks on different sides of the same room — 93
    path to recovery — 96
    chalk — 98
    pillars of creation — 99
    stepping out — 100
    i'm sorry, stephen — 103
    sandwich board — 104
    summer evenings on public transport — 105
    the man with a lance in his chest — 106
    a bouquet for alan in lieu of being able to do anything meaningful — 108
    oh, romeo — 110
    what you deserve — 111
    body swap secrets — 112

fertiliser

the hand that pulls the line	117
brid	118
a certain summer	120
no more gruel	121
cut me open	122
soundtrack to a life: a certain trigger	124
in and out	125
dance, darling	126
off-balance	128
dinosaur skeleton	130
generation game, family fortunes et al.	132
standing in the filth	133
what's yours is mine	134
made from trees	135
...and flow	136
painting glass jars	138
chalk part II	140
yumbo	141
sonnet of gentle reflections	142
soundtrack to a life: high as hope	143
mother	144
close your eyes and think of flåm	146
sleeping lessons part II	150
iron man 3: a christmas film released in april	151
autumn brings the ghosts	152
bicep stain	154
cheap waltzers	155
555	156
it's never really night time	162
soundtrack to a life: wall of arms	163
the living building	164
███████ make ████████ sculptures	166
nothing to be happy about	167

acknowledgements / notes	169
about the author / about the publisher	173

all the rot

dirt

the sleeping man

When the world finally
Departs
And leaves my mind at ease for
One
Brief
Moment, I am treading water
In the tranquil calm for mere minutes
Before my thoughts go to the night the world ended.
I hold hands with the sleeping man
A mimic of the metal he lays on
And while away the night.
And while away every night.

wait

My unbearable lightness holds me
at the top of the scales
makes it difficult
when weight after weight stacks in my trembling arms

They take the skin from my nose
from my chin
and pull the platform down below the teetering edge

Each weight sits perfectly on top of the last
to make a tower rising over my head
that pushes me down as it grows
until its peak sits where my feet started

Dropping further still
the other side of the scale comes up to meet me,
he is there at eye level
but the weight of time blocks my eyes
and I can pretend this is the reason
they don't meet

A moment of breathlessness
cradling helplessness
disguises itself as weightlessness
for longer than its measure until
another compression of my spine
drops me lower,
the brief equilibrium passes unceremoniously

He rises out of view
and I yearn for unbearable lightness
to catch me like it used to,
before every scraped shin and grazed knee
left their indelible marks
on my insides

We move in different ways
despite travelling the same direction,
so as my knees buckle
as my fingers bleed
as my ankles crack
under the months and years,
I lie to myself that there'll be nothing to fear
when the stack of stone stops growing
when the chain pulls taut
when I reach the bottom

All I need to do is wait

burst ventricle, broken heart

there's a hole in my heart
about the right size for a tongue
      to worm its way through the valves,
      drop the core of my organ
      through the void in my chest
and slowly break apart the flesh
within the blood red apple
      while what it can't bear to eat
      rots away around it

    there's a hole in my heart
    about the right size for a shot glass
          to fit like a plug
          like a cup holder
          like a blockage,
uncork me and pour the contents
to sterilise my chambers
      the perfect decanter to let
      someone else breathe

      there's a hole in my heart
      about the same size as a coin slot
          pour in your gold
          for the piggy to hold
until the time comes for
you to take the porcelain
      delicately in both hands with a
      greedy smile and crack it
like cheap Easter chocolate
      to take back all you put in

there's a hole in my heart
about the same size as a fist
    but it's hard to tell when
    the edges are frayed like petals
    chewed jagged by the teeth of insects
ripped and torn and stretched
with no way to stitch them back
    together without my life leaking
    through and staining the rest of me,
        making parts stick
        that ought to move freely
            so instead the tattered maw
            lies in wait between my lungs
        for something to engulf
        something to wrap around
        something to close it up
            and allow it to function
            because it needs permission first

with every bite of every fruit

My teeth pierce the skin and tear away at the flesh beneath.
I stubbornly revel in the sweetness of the body
filling me up until I've chewed all the flavour out
and I'm left with mulch in my mouth.

I take another bite, and another,
adamant I'm going to enjoy the next one, ignoring the
bitterness of the juice running down my chin and the
sourness of the pith caught between my teeth.
Surely the next bite of the sweet flesh will wipe away the
aftertaste.
This next bite will be nothing but sweet.

I try not to think about the juice that's dried and cracked my chin,
left it sticky for the swarming flies. Or about the shards
of skin stabbing my gums like knives. Each time
I take a bite of the fruit I leave behind a patch of blood.
Surely this next bite will be sweet.

energy cannot be destroyed, only changed

As I fall down, the soil and worms find their way
into my mouth but I am not there to spit them out.
Slowly but surely I return to the earth like an

ice cube left in a metal sink on a cold day
but I am not there to gather myself back up.
I melt, I dissolve, I crumble, I decay.

People weep, people grieve, they shed a tear. They
remember me, fleetingly, as something puts my ghost
further in the backs of their minds until eventually,

when I stop passing through lips or thoughts
at all, I die my second and final death
and wherever I go is all that's left of me.

three flies on the severed head of a mouse

Summer comes at a time when I've never been happier, so naturally I wonder which seam it's about to pull with its sticky summer fingers. The family next door are out in full force, three generations filling the garden with bodies and sound that spill from their confines – a gas leak, a broken water pipe diluting the sticky afternoon. Between the patio and the astroturf our feet find no sanctuary from burning. I keep mine up against the chair and squint at the colours bursting from the wooden planters. The sun warms our exposed skin in a time when I've never been happier, and I am pulled away from the sun kissing my skin when you point to a sticky summer finger pulling on a seam.

Several days before the heatwave begins we are greeted by a mouse in our living room. It's the first time one of our cats has brought back anything still living and even though it tries to play dead on our rug I can see it breathing when I get the chance to look up close. You want to release it where it won't instantly be caught again, so we manage to corral the faux corpse into a cardboard box and take a walk in the park across the road. On the way down to the tulip garden there's a trail off the main path. When I open the lid to check on our friend there's a split second where he flops from upright back to a corpse, and he stays in this pose when we place him in the on the undergrowth until long after we give him some space, but I still catch the movement of his breath. I fold the cardboard box and put it in the bin at the bottom of the slope.

Several days after the heatwave begins, our other cat decides to join the fun and chases another mouse back and forth along the back fence. I grab him by the scruff of his neck to end his games and bring him inside. The last time I catch a glimpse of the mouse it disappears behind a planter in the back corner of the garden. With a cat under my arm I close the curtains to keep the heat away.

And on this day in between, this liminal space sandwiched by scurrying mice, in a time when I've never been happier, you point to something on our plastic grass. Between the mice that got away there is one who wasn't lucky enough for us to intervene. There is nothing but its head. At least the eyes are closed in some sort of false dignity. I look at it through cheap Primark sunglasses while the straw in my mouth slowly delivers tequila sunrise behind my teeth. I keep sipping as three flies in turn land on the head, astronauts coming to mine the comet, some respite in endless space. Part of me wants to throw the head over the fence into next door's garden but that's probably the grenadine talking. Instead I leave it one more day and when I go to dispose of it with a pinch of paper towel, I have to wrestle it from the cat who has taken to play with it like the countless toys he ignores. I'll never know what became of those other two mice but here, at a time when I've never been happier, I clutch tightly to all that's left of something dead.

if i gave you an orchard, you'd go mad

Half-swallowed by greenery
on the blind turn of a country road,
a faded hand-painted sign
welcomes apple pickers
to turn in a mile further down

I inch closer
to the passenger window,
try to make you glance my way
but your eyes stay on the road
stoic and static
even though I know
by the flicker of your eyebrow
my movement caught your periphery

For the next two minutes
we dance this dance,
both of us thinking the other is leading,
both of us refusing to follow our cues

You don't know that I know
that you know that I know,
while I am infallible and know
your every move
but keep up the pretence

A surprise trip to the orchard
we pass by every time
you take me
home, hand picking fruit
we bake into a pie
and laugh in the kitchen
with our noses delicately smudged with flour
like a romantic comedy

For those two minutes
I let myself live in an
episode of I Love Lucy
because in this
one-sided dance
an apple is too much
for you
while I have to stop myself
ripping the trees from their roots
and placing them at your feet

After the turning
disappears behind us
I can't keep up the pretence;

I have apples
in the fridge at home

horoscope funeral

The consequence of a long life
is to create volumes of anecdotes
with few people left to hear them.
In the front row I am handed words
as empty as the pews behind me.

I am listening to generics,
a hasty message in a birthday card
for a colleague I've never met,
a copy-and-paste corporate apology
that skirts the issue and never actually apologises,
a horoscope buried in a Sunday tabloid
that's the right amount of vague but affirming
for enough people to consider it relevant.

Anyone could be inside the coffin
resting ten feet from my face.
The words keep coming through a tin can
on the end of a piece of string,
being spun out by a phonograph
whose needle keeps slipping
and no one to set it right.

small

Look me square in my closed eyes,
do everything you can to coerce
and convince me to believe the lies

He visits me sometimes and tries –
we both do – to ignore the night time curse
so looks me square in my closed eyes

Constellations conspire and let us revise
the script, so we sit and we rehearse
and I try to convince myself to believe the lies

We both sit through this torment in the guise
of long lost love, despite how much it hurts
to look him square in his closed eyes

Soon enough the morning will chastise
me and revel in making me feel worse
so please convince me to believe the lies

There can only ever be one sun rise
and I cannot compete with the universe.
Look me square in my closed eyes
I'm on my knees begging to believe the lies.

winter sun

a man shivers and covers his eyes in his sleep
while Winter Sun next to him sits upright and plays
with the frayed embroidery of a pillow case,
contemplating how he can melt through the window
and into the night like the breath that carried their names –
heavy, heated, impermanent.

the shivering man grunts under the glare as he squints through
one eye and asks if everything is okay, Winter Sun brushes him off,
watches the stranger go back to sleep and
waits for the tell-tale snores to know he's alone again.

Winter Sun slides from the bed,
quiet and smooth as the words that got him in it. He grabs at
his constellation of belongings on the trodden carpet,
clutches his keys to stifle their song, bleeds through
door after door. The stranger, still asleep, sighs away the tension
with a deep breath that can't be seen.

the Morse code of the elevator light goes unanswered,
and within its empty vowels and consonants Winter Sun
watches himself dress in the mirror. The encounter is undone
in the time it takes to hit the ground, his own private showing
picking the orange peel from the floor and fixing it back
to his stringy white pith.

the height of summer brings uncharacteristic warmth
to the night. the sun chasing its own tail denies true darkness
from the one place that asks it and dusk bleeds
over into to dawn, stretching the night like chewing
gum until it sits translucent and timeless over Winter Sun
as he presses into the soft tarmac with each step as
hard as he dares. With no fear of turning to
salt, it runs in tears off his back, ignored.

he's already forgotten which house he came from, every house
on every street looks the same, and he knows he'll never return
after getting what he was wanted, but the power of fusion doesn't
last, the more he creates the more he needs, consuming from
within. already he's glazing over himself to find more faces
covering their eyes to shield from him.

he doesn't take the time to read names

the cruel face of lazarus

Worse than the dreams where
nothing was ever wrong
are the ones where we still
lost you to the undergrowth,

where the hardened flakes of
pot-pourri still dropped through the
hourglass years at a time like
flocks of swans falling from the sky

and I still took the time to mourn,
only to walk through the front
door of the house that's no longer ours
and see you standing there

like nothing has been wrong
all this time, and even though we're both
farthest from the truth we ignore the
rancid screech of the elephant and I

am wary that doing the wrong thing
will return you to the undergrowth
that has sprouted thick and dark from
the eggshells I force myself to walk on.

the stranger in my grandad's coffin

Decades of working in a sheet metal factory ended
with nails picked clean at the end of leathery labourer's fingers
that I only ever saw through a layer of dirt or grime.

I reach out for the alien, pedicured hand and find no warmth.
The heart, the soul, the skin, sitting icily in my palm like a photocopy,
a reconstruction of something familiar that isn't quite right.
The flawlessly even complexion from forehead to chin
belongs to someone else, too, taking away his character and leaving
behind the face of someone flat and...

He waits in a suit and tie
– an outfit I'd only seen him wear a handful of times –
and I worry this last image will override the memories of him
wearing one of his gravy-stained polo shirts. I slip my note
into his pocket, apologising for not being as present
as I could have been in recent years.

It's mostly to assuage my own guilt, seeing as though he wasn't
going to be reading it any time soon, and finishes
with the consolation that he is reunited with his son,
again placating my own fears that there's more to the universe
than becoming an urn on a mantelpiece.

I bungee between his coffin and the door,
screaming as I plunge,
knowing the facsimile will be resigned to memory
once the elastic gives up.

ebb...

The vast expanse begs I take its proffered hand
to show me the unknown possibilities I could have
achieved. With arms open wide
I am pulled in, surrounded by everything I ever
held close. I watch as piece by piece
twists and breaks with electric uncertainty
against the line that ebbs and flows at my feet.
Another world sits on the other side,
makes the hairs on my arms stand on end.
The maelstrom fills my lungs and
from the precipice of shadow,
the lightless and indiscernible horizon
burns my chest. I weave towards
the edge of the shore where the hard line
threatens to remain unknown. A static life on
ankle-deep potential, the furthest I'll ever go
into the open expanse, I am standing in
my own way. Lies in my future – I can see
there is nothing stretching out into the dark
despite the whispers in my ear
and I return to thoughts I can call my own.
The cinder blocks beneath me in the sand
call to bind my wrists and ankles within
constricting openness – makes me lose that fleeting
chance to be calm with it. Only

giving me a small window to try and grasp any
of the contents rolling around inside my head,
the overwhelming and seemingly endless crashing
of the waves coming up to meet me overtakes
my mind. In place of my thoughts, white noise –
a stone sits in the centre of an empty room, in-
capable of changing anything. More often than not
thread after thread after thread
sway in the wind over the edge of the world
where unseen fingers unravel the town, until empty
promises of what could be possible tug
the stitching of the cliffs at my back.
When all form is taken away from the hem of
my world, the sand shifts in ways I that can't
keep up with what I want to achieve. For
where only a wish can carry me out
I am here, slowly eroding away on an empty beach.

legacy

Uncinched waist wants to unravel free from
panicked fingers that spend too much time gathering
their loose skin to keep the flow of sand at bay

The hourglass sits on the shelf still counting time
that falls through its chipped ribcage, lands loose in the knots
of varnished wood, pours over the edge, gravity all it knows

A lack of petrichor brings the rain unannounced, a hastily
placed plastic bucket catches the drops, each grain taunting how
everything you ever were sits in the hands of someone else.

measuring catastrophic events

You can see them at the beach sometimes
as if someone dragged a rake across the cliff side

    lines through the rock

If you understand the language of the lines
they can tell you when they sat at
the bottom of the ocean
or when the ocean came up to them
or when fire swept the land and they slept under
    a blanket of trees collapsed and crushed into charcoal
or when volcanic activity blocked out the sun and
    made the land barren

If you understand the language of the lines
they can share their history and how long
each catastrophe took to rear its head

    my fingers are chewed down
    to where they are raw painful

If you understand the language of the lines
you can tell the last time I sat
at the bottom of the ocean

do you hear that memory?

You think you're remembering exactly
how it happened when in fact
each recall only reaches
as far as the one that came before,

not intricately
tracing the picture beneath but
turning the page and starting
again with each rendition
softening the curves
a little.

The curse of loving
a point in time
is to know less
of its shape whenever you
roll it through your hands,
to smooth it out
a little more with every touch,

where cherishing something
puts it in jeopardy
and, behold, the irony that
the only way to keep
it intact
is to let go of it completely.

Do you hear that memory?
You think you do, but the sound
is the first to go.
He's laughing,
you're certain,
but it can't find your ears.

Neither does the way
he says your name
nor the songs he sings in the shower.
And all you can do is
wear away
at what was, like how

the wind slowly
beats the mountain as the erosion
of the rock pulls you
further
and further away
from the summit where you
planted your flag

a table set for four

once I am swallowed and sieved into pieces
and time calls on me to dig my trench, I will find
myself in a dining chair
at a dining table
in a dining room

there's no way to tell what day it's going to be
but I do know
the table is set for four and the smell of garlic
fills the room
my lungs
my soul
just as much as the laughter

and for a change I don't mind that I'm pinned
between the table and the radiator
because it's a warmth I've missed
for oh so long,
long enough to make me question
whether or not my
recreation is
entirely accurate

trade network

Seventeen teeth wane a crescent into my forearm,
a cuneiform dental record – an ancient precursor
to everything that spilled out into a world where we bite
down on coins because we can't allow others in
without impressing ourselves into their offerings.

The mark on my arm fades; the gap between my
golden bones posits the closest to a passing fancy
on this softening body that slowly loses its distinction
under the pressure of its own curdling. I am left

alone where waxing indents are the only currency in a
market I have no desire to be consumed by. I tell myself
this lie while my fingers trace my depreciating worth.

ocean moth

an arm around my waist keeps
      my decayed vessel buoyant,
afloat above the chequerboard floor
swirling with the light and tide,
      the push and pull of a humid ocean

the congregation moves as one
to the sermon from the strobe-lit pulpit
like a hive mind
      a colony
      a collection of conformity
rotted skin pushes through
      breaks the waves
tongues crash against bleeding rocks
under rich purples and starving greens

      our soft bellies press close
to not be exposed to sharp onlookers
you pull me closer
      away from the waves
your buckle digs into my carcass but
metal tastes sweeter than salt
I dig in my heels, my nails
      feel the flesh give like citrus

you whisper a storm
over open water that hits my ear like
a breeze on the shore and carries me away
      on a gingham raft

we cocoon it around ourselves
melt into an indistinguishable chrysalis to
emerge not knowing how much of our decomposition
      returned to its rightful home

      I leave with your sourness on my lips
but then lime was always

                      my favourite flavour

i have no body

it would appear I have this
unquenchable need to fix myself
into something that could almost

be something else if you squint
fleetingly through the foliage
of the shy canopy and look

at me through the smoke
and mirrors I have arranged
amongst the dense clay trees.

my malleable self has learnt
it as a way of defence, twisting
the form into whatever offers

the least resistance and most
satisfaction as long as it's
kept at arm's length to avoid

the detection that it's a mismatch,
forced together with nothing to
keep the seams from falling apart.

instead I can remain attractive
to the people who don't get
close enough to notice how I'm

jammed together, or my texture
isn't what it should be for my
form, like they've eaten something

sweet but wince at my sourness
and balk at the other people's
fingerprints still shaping me.

ship of theseus

plank by plank,
piece by piece,
me by me,
Theseus seizes a part and hands back
something identical to go in its place

Through time, through experience,
through biology, I'm not the person I was
five   ten   fifteen
years ago, but I should still be me.

So then I try to unfold the concept of me
the concept of self
the concept of being defined by
a consciousness left in the past
waiting in the future
lingering in the present
to be all of those all at once and never again.

Theseus first looks at me
in my new, identical image,
then over to the other corner where enough of my original
discarded parts have been rebuilt
into a new, identical image.

He looks at us both and doesn't know
which one to believe when both of us say we're real.
He is not alone.

sleeping lessons

Kept company until the sun comes up by the BBC programmes about learning another language that you record onto VHS tapes with the intention of going back and picking up Japanese when you're more lucid but never do, wasting the tapes because you're so sure of yourself you take off that little tab to make the contents permanent.

    Soon you forget about your inability to sleep because you mask your insomnia by burning the candle at both ends, blaming your terrible sleep pattern on working late shifts, studying beyond necessity and enjoying nights out intense enough to immediately collapse on the bed still fully clothed.

    Adulthood hits and you find yourself needing to go to bed sober at a reasonable hour only for the deafening chatter to return as soon as your head hits the pillow, so you throw the television on and fall asleep to the distraction of canned laughter to familiar sitcom zingers, usually setting the sleep timer but sometimes forgetting, waking to the *Friends* theme on loop hours later.

obsessions with black hole theories

i.

I don't remember where, or when, or by whom, but I once heard the supposition of death having an inverted event horizon. It could be a terrifying notion depending on how we end up leaving the coil but I ended up finding comfort in the idea that a person can get closer and closer to the line but never cross it as their perception of time gradually ceases to exist. So while an outsider observes the end, I guess I liked the idea that on some level in, some form of perception, you haven't gone away.

ii.

an object of light and warmth
extinguished too early into its lifespan
collapsed into a primordial black hole

what was there is gone forever
but what takes its place has such
vast gravity it holds together
everything it left behind

iii.

It's impossible to know because this is its very nature, but the idea an entire universe sits inside a black hole is at all times fascinating, terrifying and frustrating in equal measure. The oldest and largest of all things in the universe, the only thing that will be left after everything else has fallen to the void, all consuming, inescapable.

The other side could house huge expanses of life or a crushing eternity of nothing. The only way to know once and for all to cross over and witness it first hand which has only ever presented itself as a one way journey thus far.

I stand in front of a black hole as it relentlessly swallows the horizon.

fan belt

                Everything is turning.
                Everything is in motion.
                Everything works,
                but not quite how it should.
                Once in a while the fan belt slips,
a brief moment out of sync,
            a cry for help from an engine
            that otherwise works fine.
            No warning lights,
            no breakdowns,
            just one part of the whole
            not behaving.

            The fan belt slips
            again and again.
            It's nothing.

            You keep driving.

limits

Whenever I find myself
in one those rare moments where I've gone
long enough without chewing my nails
down to where my fingers are bloody and painful,
they'll reach the stage
where I can bend them back and forth,
and since I lack impulse control so completely -
coupled with a compulsion to push everything to its limit -
I'll keep doing it over and over
and over
until the nail finally bows to the pressure and tears away
down to where my fingers are bloody and painful.

Every single pen I own
has had that little plastic tab pulled off
from when I would bend it back and forth,
and since I lack impulse control so completely
I always went that little bit further
to where the plastic faded and split
like the fibres of a nail
and screamed when it finally gave way.

None of my milk teeth
came out on their own terms,
twisted and torn bloody
from frayed gums because neither my finger
nor my tongue could just leave them be.

Or that crack heard from the back
of the classroom because
the words "shatter-proof" were printed
on my misshapen ruler
as an issue of challenge
which gave me no option to accept,
my excuse after I snapped my
fifth one of the month.

This urge I have for
just a little more,
just a little longer,
seeing how much pushback something can take
before I push it too far.

A pen. A tooth.
A nail. A ruler.
My phone as I walk by the canal.
My tentative relationships with others.
The edge of the platform at the train station.

visitation at the infinite prison

When I take my seat
at the partition the stool
is crooked and I need to adjust its height
to make sure my face aligns with the
drawings she's made
on the glass.
As we talk I play the part she's given me
with all its bells and whistles,
and at some point
during the conversation
I start believing
the face she's drawn
for me is my own.

When I move to the next window
he's done the same thing,
drawn on the glass
to give me features when I sit opposite.
He talks to these features instead of to me,
and in a desperate attempt at
connection I try to make my face
what he's looking for,
copying what he wants
in the hopes of being seen.

The line stretches on.
Each interaction kept behind a
sheet of glass marked by lines
that edit my face
to my visitor's desire.
I play every part with gusto,
and to make sure I do it well enough
I draw that face over my own
and embody an unrecognisable
cubist patchwork,
but still each visit comes to an end.

After sitting in front of so many
sheets of glass,
I find myself in front of one
with no markings.
At first I think it's a mistake
but he sees me.
He sees my face, my real face
free from lines that were
traced to please other people,
and through the clear glass
I can see him,
for the first time I can see
the person on the other side
of the glass without
expectations getting in the way.

unrequited

A woman somewhere in her seventies made eyes at me across the table and even though I tried to carry on as though I didn't notice I could see her in the corner of my eye, looking me up and down with an unmistakable hunger. She sat a little straighter and laughed like a schoolgirl at my every word, and when she tried to play footsie with me I scooted my chair back surreptitiously to hide that she was making her way up my calf as much as her elderly flexibility allowed.

I was told this could happen but didn't grasp the full extent until ten minutes earlier when the words *You know who this is* – delivered neither as question nor statement but somewhere in the exasperated between space – were met with a bewildered shake of the head.

It's a hard thing when a face that helped raise you looks back at you like you're a stranger. The woman who made hot chocolate on Saturday nights before bed and watery porridge for breakfast the next morning looked at me through eyes that thought we were the same age. No more laughing at misplaced keys or looking for glasses that were already on her head. No more worrying about escaping the house where she lived for half a century and getting lost because the flame that once shone so very bright has burned and burned its way deep down into the impenetrable well of wax.

Seeing a storm of a woman being quelled by time is too much. I want to grab her and shake her and scream in her face to remember me but instead I sit at the table and ignore her advances, say goodbye, and cry on the car ride home.

cassandra

Atlantis ignores each tide creep further up its shores
and I am Cassandra looking back at myself through the mirror.
There's an urge to speak the way of things,
a desire to let the curtain slip
but the words would fall like unwelcome rain
and seep into ground too afraid it will buckle under the damp.
Do you know what it is to drown?
To truly be swallowed by the sea?
I've seen it happen; the rush of something other than air,
a place so deep and cold no light can reach,
to only know which way is up by watching life escape.
In the harsh light of day a bed becomes a shroud
wrapped around the heart of Atlantis,
we sink with it like stones
and I am Cassandra looking back at myself through the mirror.

i used to like museums but now i'm not so sure

A stranger came around and built a grand museum well beyond the confines of my garden, even though I never asked for him to do as such. And when it was complete he showed the plaque above the door which bore my name ornately carved in stone as if it came from Ancient Rome. He cut the rope and ushered me inside, the first to see the opulence that I would not have chosen had I been consulted on the matter.

My eyes then caught the floor plan where the horrible discovery was made that every exhibition bore my name just like the ornate plaque above the door. The rooms were filled with memories my preference would have been to leave behind – instead they stretched from floor to ceiling marked with footnotes of excruciating depth.

I never asked to have this building raised, I never asked to have my name adorn a plaque above its door or fill its halls, yet here it was – displayed upon request by everyone who wasn't me so they could judge if I was living in a way society would deem acceptable, because we need to package every part of our existence, leaving warts and all to be displayed.

And when the patron asks about a piece I hadn't noticed I'm expected to acknowledge their concern despite the fact I didn't even know I needed it until they pulled the rug from underneath my feet.

There is a room, just one, I like to spend my time, because it's filled with exhibitions that I chose to occupy the space, the ones I want to reminisce about and not have forced upon my calendar of consciousness by those with good intentions but whose names do not adorn the plaque above the door.

divergence and fault

We were green together, stretching our
Hands out to the opening world, taking in
Everything for the first time,
New eyes, new hands, new tongues.

Winter was an age away, our youth was
Eternal and stretched out before us,
Reaching beyond what we saw and knew.
Eagerly we pushed onwards

To explore the lands of ourselves and each
Other in intimate detail. Monuments to our
Greatness scraped the heavens with
Entwined fingers and tongues and limbs,
Telling the world who we were with our
Hearts finally on our sleeves,
Engraved with promises made of moss,
Renewal, and the acceptance of being seen.

Inevitably, youth's folly caught up

With us, just how eventually
It catches up with every reckless
Spring fire that burns with the wrong fuel,
Heating up until it's entirely consumed by

Its own misguided iridescence and we
Make the realisation all too late that sowing

Seeds in the same season won't always make
Orchards grow. And so the lands that forged
Mountains when they came together pull the
Earth apart. Continents filled
With unstoppable resolve gave in to
Habit and drifted away from each other, forming
Estuaries that widened into oceans filled with
Razor sharp words that tore into the flesh of
Everything trying its hand at survival.

Even the monuments we thought would
Last forever have no worshippers left to
See them crumble with the coast, joining the
Eroded stones of the seabed.

a second earthquake would have been less memorable

A bed on wheels
and I wake up dead
centre of the room, my brain
on slow-start confused
because my eyes opened to
the wrong image.
It remains unfamiliar,
regardless of how many
times the wind is pulled
away in strands,
being pushed aside
for the inescapable
fate of inconsequentiality –
being a background extra for
another protagonist
while the camera
lingers on them
for a wide shot that
traps you in frame, a prisoner
laughing empty air as your
limbs lose feeling.
One night, I learned
what it meant for a stomach
to turn. My bed on
wheels stuck hard
and fast in its corner,
but still my eyes
opened to a wrong
image – an image of slanted

laughter pooling into
swamps of quicksand where
each squeak of
leather and rubber
burned the fibres
swirling at the back of my
neck until they made
holes to chafe my skin
raw. And even long
after the lights have died,
the stiffness in my
joints wends its
black and blue
fingers through my
sinew, a chromatography
boasting how a sweetness
permeates the dull
thrombosis and I listen
to this bravado
because there's no one
to yell "Cut!" and
let me know the cameras
have stopped
so we can reset and try
again and live in
blissful, naive hope that
if things go right
this time, I'll wake up dead
centre of the room again.

helicopter

I opened my eyes and found him where he shouldn't be; yet there
he was above all things as though he, like the heretic,
had not to my very face denounced me thrice.
So I asked him, for I needed an answer, "Prithee,
tell me how you expect to imbibe the ichor
of my veins when you recoil
at the idea of my body being the pitcher?"
To wit, he turned to me – "Can a man not allow a recipe
close to his heart should he not like its writer? Or is the piece
lost to the loose end of a swinging rope
hanging from the edge of an angel's perch?"

broken things make for gorgeous sculptures

I cannot stop the itching in the spaces where my fingers meet
and this is all I can think about when a perfect
pastel gradient tries to convince me it's over.
I know I have come to an end and I welcome it – want it, even –
but I fall deeper into where my skin chips away
like flakes of paint defeated by rust
purely because something is trying to make that decision for me.
Lacklustre birdsong fails
to punctuate the featureless blue because I have
taken it upon myself to pluck the wilting notes from the air
and store them behind my eyes until I can get the radio to work.

Long ago I had a purpose, different to the one I have now.
It sits on the periphery of my memory
under a haze of gasoline fumes and burnt rubber –
it's there but intangible, so I am resigned to my current state,
a state I haven't quite figured out beyond forming
an aesthetic for the enjoyment and consumption of others.

Pressed against another who has found
the same emptiness spilling forth from within,
we pull each other too close,
we break and warp our marrowed chassis until they
                                        sew together into each other,
we share the purpose we still don't fully understand
as we both ignore how the gradient tries to pry us apart.

decomposition

finding the gate that takes me home

I spent too much time clamped shut
fumbling through the bracken trying to find
that fabled place where the branches waltz around
themselves and open up the room.

They waited for me under the dazzling sun
as my world turned pink and drew me nearer
to the soft leaves adorning the twisted wreath
And with my clumsy hands ball-fisted
like a child clutching its mother's hair
I peel myself apart and look back at the trail I walked.

superstitious limbs

The space between, it pulls you in
to keep the fates at bay,
while overhead the roof of limbs
attempts to lead the way.

A gentle rapping on the bones
was once enough to sate,
but evermore the rotting stones
demand more on their plate.

A crunch of death beneath the feet
might feel like sedition,
but gods so love their irony
alongside superstition.

peculiar behaviour

If you were to look down you might see a boy
stumble his way through the forest,
tripping over gnarled roots hidden in the undergrowth
like the monster's hand reaching from under the bed

If you were to look down you might see the boy
as he walks, but catch him a man in the fleeting
moments his path winds through the dappled light
before the shade snatches him back to boyhood

If you were to look down you might find it peculiar
how the boy places a hand against every tree,
and with each suitable trunk he tears at the skin
of his knuckles only for no one to respond

And if you were to look down you might also find it peculiar
that each tree has a figure behind, hiding from the boy,
mirroring his steps in a silent dance around the trunks
to remain undetected by the visitor

a place to sit

He swings the axe
He swings the axe

Sweat pours from his brow
A jagged smile creeps into the trunk
happy with the work he is doing

He swings the axe

The job is tough
Sweat pours from his brow
When he is done he will have a seat

He swings the axe
The jagged smile grows wider
Sweat pours from his brow

He swings the axe
happy with the work he is doing
Sweat pours from his brow

He needs a place to sit and rest
The job is tough
He swings the axe

The job is tough
He needs a place to sit
When the tree tilts its head back in raucous laughter
his job will be done
And he will have a place to sit
And recover from the job

The job is tough

He swings the axe
He swings the axe
He swings the axe

something to crush in the rain

I do not wish to venture beyond the forest
and out of protection from the rain
so I nestle with my back against the rough bark,
held between two roots like a child in a mother's loving embrace

At least, that's the lie I tell myself.
While it's true the rain is an inconvenience
I stay because the wood hasn't offered
a satisfactory answer to the question I was
too afraid to properly ask but
for which I still expected closure

So I sit stubbornly at the edge of the tree line
telling myself I'll get up when the rain eases,
secretly wishing for a storm that lasts longer
than the silence of the trees as I grab fistfuls
of leaves and crush them into powder
before they turn too sodden and malleable

nesting time

Birdsong.
    It's time to wake up.
I cough up feathers as the tickle in my throat
    grows too unbearable.
There's a bird's nest in front of me and I don't
    know how it got there.
Each mote of dust
    hatches into a different bird.
It looks too pristine, placed delicately on the dirty ground,
    like cartoon twigs sticking out at perfectly jumbled angles.
Looking at my own mouth, each tooth is rounded and mottled –
    brittle eggs that chip and crack when I clench my jaw.
The nest is filled with my teeth-eggs, and the egg I purloined
    dissolves on my tongue and pours into my hourglass stomach.
There definitely wasn't a bird's nest when I sat down,
    it's something I would have remembered.
I reach into the nest,
    pull out an egg and feel its shell give way against my teeth.
A fluttering of wings doubles me over,
    my cry of discomfort comes out as a squawk.
Pieces of shell stick in my tongue and my gums,
    in the back of my throat. Yolk oozes from the wounds.
Birds and painful laughter
    fly from my mouth at a troubling rate.
It's time to wake up.

waste as medicine

Aches caught in the cracks of a crumbling husk
Threads of promises left to dangle and fray in a storm
Faded print on yellowed paper

A prison's throne stands tall above a
kingdom of hoarded clutter,
a hollow rule forged and forced in chains.

Keep the statue in the plaza,
a monument to love's perseverance,
but gather up the rotting, discoloured bouquets from its base,
gather up the soft toys with their veins of mould,
gather up the vestiges of reverence long since stripped of dignity

Know the value of what to keep
gather up the rest
throw it out.

still

Your heart still beats in my chest
with a coarseness that scratches my
lungs, and sometimes still I spend
sleepless nights lost in your sleepless city.
Sometimes still your feet fill my shoes and
your air fills my lungs as they itch next to your beating heart,
and soon you're making your way through my veins
like a guest who's outstayed their welcome,
someone somewhere they shouldn't be,
but who I still can't bring myself to ask to leave.
I feel my shirt sticking to my back,
the ink from my book blemishes
my finger tips, my shoulder presses into another
that will not find its way home with me in these sleepless nights.
Nor will your shoulder that I still think to lean on
while I spend my hours awake in a bed half
damp with sweat and half uncreased and perfect,
because you spend all you can coursing through me.
And yet still, despite you being in my chest
in my shoes
                    in my lungs
                                        in my veins
being in all the wrong places,
to consider it wrong feels wrong and I resign myself
to a coarse heartbeat whose rhythm I cannot
predict and still gives me sleepless nights.

little lobster boy

Lobsters, in theory, are immortal.
Which is to say
they don't degenerate as they age,
but eventually die of exhaustion
when their shells
need too much energy
                      to shed.

I'm thinking about this fact
when you're on my bed
and I'm at my desk
trying to get the ancient laptop to send
something to the ancient printer,
because, as the youngest child,
I've automatically acquired
the mantle of IT Support.

There's been a knot
caught in my throat
for the better part of half
a year and I can feel it
      swelling
with each conversation
we don't have,
and if it gets any bigger
I'll have to
claw at my neck
just to breathe.

It's agitating.
The more I want to say something
the harder it gets
to open my mouth
because the moment that passed
was adequate enough
but so is the moment coming up
so stop being precious and just go for it
and I'm screaming in my head
to open the valve
while trying to get the printer to
feed the paper through.

You look at me
like you know I have
something to say,
and I'm pretty sure
you already know
                     because a mother always knows
and in eighteen years
of being your son
I've never been able to get
anything by you.

Finally I push
it up from my throat
like an engorged slug
with slime that coats my tongue,
that keeps me from saying
the actual words,
so instead I settle
for a euphemism and tell you
I'm seeing one of my friends.
 Seeing seeing

one of my friends.

And at that moment I am
on the sea floor.
I am on my back,
    prone,
        exhausted.
Completely exposed
without any
protection.
And I know your love is
unconditional,
I knew that even before
you had one less
output for it,
and I know I've been
very lucky in that respect,
but still,
I am on my back,
    prone,
        exhausted.

You've been waiting
for me to tell you,
much longer than just this evening,
　　　　　　　　　just this conversation,
and your tears hitting my shoulder
while you hold me close
feel more like relief
that I've finally
been able to get it out there,
like you could always
see the knot caught in my throat
all this time.

When the printer finally
starts to do what it's told
I ask if you
can tell my sister for me,
because while
lobsters don't degenerate with age,
they eventually die of exhaustion
when their shells
　　　　　need too much energy
　　　　　　　　　　　　to shed.

water off a duck's back

> *"Words can't hurt you, only your own perception of those words."*
> Jinkx Monsoon

Sticks and stones
may break my bones
but words will
leave scars of the emotional and
psychological kind that are
much harder to overcome

one time I was told our brains
ignore when our organs itch because
it would drive us insane and I wondered
how many scratches it would take
for me to get through the skin
satisfy the ocean depths
feel everything
after my own subconscious decided to lie

scar tissue on the soul
never stops itching
and I was too far gone below the waves
fingers too pruned and useless to
rend the skin from my flesh
rend the flesh from my bones
to rip at my own heart
scratch the tissue and lift from this beast
the burdens of someone else's design

but what is a scar
if not proof of strength? Proof
that wounds close and heal
a memento of resilience
through struggle

and when I return to the surface
with hardened claws I will
fight the urge
rumbling down my spine
and I will not open a wound
of my own
instead each itch will be its own
heartbeat letting me know
that I'm alive

hometown magnification

There's no home left in my hometown
The only house I ever knew has strangers
tripping over the creaky step
listening to the boiler hum
in the corner of the bedroom
pulling their dogs away from chewing
at the fibreglass panels in the kitchen

I look at the house on Google Maps
there's a car in the driveway
I don't recognise

But the street view picture is old
and I see a familiar *Beware the Dog* sign
on the fence
and I see a familiar basket hanging from
the wrought iron hook out front
and I see a familiar white ball that, when I wrote on it,
    made my mum see a ghost
and I see a familiar collection of ornaments on the living room
                                                                    windowsill
beneath a familiar tasselled blind

I spend time in that one spot
spinning the camera to see everything I knew,
from my earliest memories
to flying the nest,
from learning to ride a bike
to coming home drunk as dawn
peaked over the rooftops

I think about how I'll never see it again
and about how it belongs to someone else.

an odd number of cycles

An odd number of candles bunched together
at one side of the fireplace, sitting on a large plate
where the wax mixes and pools in a nebula

An odd number of fingers on an odd number of arms
beneath a tree, wrapped in a slab

An odd number of tent poles sticking out
at awkward angles where the wind has pulled them
kicking and screaming from the hooks in the soaking ground

An odd number of stones to hop across
a babbling brook except when the summer breeze
calls for paddling

An odd number of prongs on an odd number of crowns
embroidered onto the breast of a polo shirt

An odd number of cars sitting outside the house

An odd number of plant pots in an odd number of clusters
on the gravel-covered front garden

An odd number of well-wishers running after the train
until there's no platform left to follow

An odd number of suitcases
in the rack above the seats

An odd number of place settings at the dining table

An odd number of teenagers queueing for
an odd number of bathrooms

An odd number on the door

An odd number of empty glasses on a mezzanine table
as talking leads to sharing a bed

An odd number of years naming other people's dogs
watching them run by the window

An odd number of keys on a chain

An odd number of handles on an odd number of doors

An odd number of candles bunched together
at one side of the fireplace, sitting on a large plate
where the wax mixes and pools in a nebula

i think we're lost

Standing in an open field I look down
at my feet and see a salmon
struggling to breathe on the grass

It's a little on the nose, I think to myself
as I watch its gills opens and close
in panic, and perceive an existential
dread in its eyes I'm not certain
they can actually convey

The salmon doesn't move,
resigned to its fate,
and with no water nearby
there's nothing I can do to help.
I stand paralysed wondering
whether to keep moving
or ease its pain

Instead I do neither and
watch the gills slow their undulating
watch the one eye pointing at me glaze over
watch the hooked mouth and hump
on its back press into the soil

Maybe I'm supposed to feel guilt
for something out of my control
but I find I'm overcome with
relief for this dying creature
so far from where
it's supposed to be

confession

Divine are the ten fingers stitched into each other,
one hand holding another under the open sky, rejoicing
each other beyond the sanctuary of safe walls. To smother
the gift is all but blasphemous, shout it loud, voicing

a love as old as the gods, regardless of the jealous gaze
piercing our hearts from the stained-glass Madonna.
This little act holds the whole world, one hand prays
against the other down the street to cries of *hosannah*.

in which i am both orpheus and eurydice

I am Orpheus. I am Orpheus as he decides he knows better than the gods themselves. I am Orpheus as he decides he knows better than the gods themselves about the complex machinations of mortality. I am Orpheus as he decides he knows better than the gods themselves about the complex machinations of mortality and fate because unfairness fell on me and only me. I am Orpheus confronting his very creators because I am worthy of exception.

I am Eurydice. I am Eurydice walking ten steps behind the one I love. I am Eurydice walking ten steps behind the one I love who won't look at me. I am Eurydice walking ten steps behind the one I love who won't look at me, talk to me or slow their pace and I don't know why. I am Eurydice, uncertain but still following.

I am Orpheus, suspicious of my victory. I am Orpheus who knows a caveat to any victory instantly makes it pyrrhic. I am Orpheus falling apart inside, knowing my actions are driven by love but hindered by hubris. I am Eurydice met with cold indifference, left to wonder how long I have been a trophy to win or a point to prove. I am Orpheus as each heavy footstep feels more and more like I am the butt of the joke. I am Eurydice with the ash of the uneven Tartarus staircase getting between my toes, under my nails, into my eyes and my lungs. I am Eurydice unable to clear my throat. I am Orpheus digging deep to find the power not to turn around, however much I want to. I am Orpheus craving reassurance. I am Eurydice craving reassurance. I am holding petty deities at their word. I am silently begging for acknowledgement. I have conviction in my motives. I have uncertainty in my motives. I am questioning what I want. I have been pushed into someone else's journey. I have pulled someone else into mine. I am climbing. I am climbing. I am climbing. I am losing control. I am craving reassurance. I turn around.

return fire

Fate broke the ceasefire
in the most unceremonious way
before it scuttled back to its hole,
leaving the old man alone
wearing a uniform for a school
that no longer existed

Meet me in the middle, he said to himself
to anyone who would listen
to nobody

He sits with a smile
but a tug at its corners is prepared
to burn down to the bone
and make the uniform fit,
if only there was a way
of cherry-picking the bullet holes

dew, inhabited

Observe the city first thing in the morning

>while the world adjusts to the light
>knowing nothing but grey in the meantime
>before the watercolours bleed across the
>canvas-like flowers opening to the sun
>
>looking like silence with opaque windows
>and leaves sitting heavily in trees

Observe the city first thing in the morning
through the beads of morning dew
a million, million lenses
on every surface
showing worlds of their own
on every surface
alerting you to who they are
on every surface

trying to make being good an unconscious bodily process

To see a salmon in a field and not walk away
with the salty aftertaste of dilated gills, dilated pupils,
dissolving the underside of my tongue,
to follow the breadcrumb scales upstream
that lie in hopeful wait for me to pick up the trail
before they soften and curl in on themselves and
sink down, down, down and be lost to the silt

To take a bird's nest from the forest floor and place it
back in the branches, away from the threat of
tooth and claw, even my own,
especially my own,
to hear the song of fruition high in the boughs
as a call to arms, rather than a callous, taunting
siren that rings out over the bared claws and
bloodied teeth that toy with the shreds of inaction

To hear the sounds of the city and understand
when they are not meant for you
when they are meant for you
when they fall somewhere in between,

To breathe in a way that opens my chest
instead of pulling it taut around shrivelled lungs

wikipedia page funeral

I stand alone awkwardly in the car park
avoiding conversations with family
members I do not recognise, who in turn
have not seen me in at least twenty-five years.
Instead, I follow the wind dance through the leaves,
dodging names I only know from faded words

in Christmas cards, dodging awkward small-talk words
fumbling out whilst waiting for the hearse to park.
Its quiet and clandestine arrival leaves
a thick atmosphere the gathered family
wades through to their seats. Accumulated years
hide behind a veneer of beech and I turn

away, my face burning hot from shame I turn
away, because all I can hear are the words
that sat heavy on top of our final years
since the day they brought you back from the park
and I was a stranger in your family
home. A television above you shows leaves

falling gracefully, they look just like the leaves
on my blue shirt or my mum's pink dress. I turn
with burning hot cheeks and watch the family
if it means I don't have to read those two words
accompanying the footage of the park
on loop above you, counting rings like they're years,

cutting you down and counting rings as if years
are the only measurement and no one leaves
a thought for the dementia or for the park-
insons and now with tears on hot cheeks I turn
to look at the one who gave such hollow words.
A man long estranged from all his family,

doesn't know a thing about his family,
is saved by a woman who put in the years,
the only one who worked to make sure the words
were more than just emotionless facts. It leaves
a burning guilt and complicitness that turn
me redder still – despite the cold, wet car park -

already I barely know the family.
I try to park the ache and think of the years
we enjoyed before the leaves started to turn.

a palmful is a body of water

Too late after a long walk
a lake makes itself known
and I am suddenly made aware
of the dryness in my throat

When I kneel at the shore
the water offers no reflection and
invites me to dive in head first for the
fastest way to quench my thirst

I politely decline, choosing to scoop
some water into my hands
where I catch my face looking back
at me before swallowing just enough

diametrically opposed clocks on different sides of the same room

My psychiatrist's office has two clocks. One hangs above the door and one sits by her computer, slouched against the wall instead of attached to it. My chair puts a clock on each side of my vision and their uneven height makes me feel like my ears are filled with water and the ground is sloped. The clock on her desk is seven minutes and twenty seconds fast. We talk about how my inability to function strains my relationships of all kinds, and what emotional support scaffolding I can (and already have) put in place to ease the burden on myself and my loved ones. We soon discover it is mostly my loved ones who have taken up the role of my emotional support scaffolding, most likely unbeknownst to them. My psychiatrist laughs when I suggest the idea of taking down the scaffolding and watching how I crumble, but stops short and hurriedly scribbles many notes when she realises it wasn't a joke.

The first time I wait while the psychiatrist tallies my Bad Brain Score (she later tells me not to call it this) the only thing punctuating the lead balloon of silence is the syncopated ticking of the two clocks fighting each other from opposite sides of the office. They are synchronised to be perfectly out of sync, a regiment in double-time. As I count seconds as a means to ignore the awkwardness I don't notice I've been counting twice as fast because it matches the gauze in my ears made from my own heartbeat, which has burrowed so deep I don't hear the doctor the first time she tells me my Bad Brain Score (don't call it this), and when she repeats it I smile and nod. She knows I have no idea what the numbers mean, even after she explains them multiple times. This will not change over the course of our time together.

We talk. Mostly about me. Mostly I talk. My psychiatrist is both delighted and mortified that I am one of her more complicated cases. She listens to me talk about the constant fidgeting and high activity levels of my childhood countered by my innate need to be a teacher's pet and fear of repercussion from authority figures.

I tell her about all the writing projects I start but never finish. I tell her about all the hints and cues I miss every day in social interactions because my brain doesn't connect the dots. I tell her how I've gone from getting top grades at school to cramming a week's worth of work into a day because Friday has arrived and I spent the other four days in a fugue state. I tell her about the night my dad died, typed out over two sheets of A4 paper – double sided – because she wanted to know how many details of the event I could recall and I took that as a challenge. I tell her about the voice screaming inside my head like a cricket in a cage, ceaselessly chirping while my body sits motionless for hours at a time, incapable of making myself move. I tell her about how hard it is to parse the idea that my rubbish should go in the bin and not sit on the side next to me. I tell her about how the later of "I'll do it later" fame never arrives. I tell her about how my anxiety and ADHD are always at odds, because I worry about being more productive but still can't do anything about it so instead I feel a guilty and useless failure, while to others I come off as lazy and complacent. I tell her how I feel like this failure every single day while crying into my face mask and steaming up my glasses.

The flanking clocks limp their way through each session, their uneven peg-legged steps following me down hazy cobbled streets. Once again she tallies my Bad Brain Score (don't call it that) and I wait in silence. The numbers are slowly going down. As little as I understand them, I know this means my brain is getting to be a little less bad as the weeks go by, but eventually they even out because my personal growth is countered by the general decline of the world at large.

After I am diagnosed and on medication, each visit also requires a check of my blood pressure. The psychiatrist tallies my Bad Brain Score (stop calling it that) and leaves the room to get my prescription ready. I am thrown into longer bouts where my only company hangs in my periphery, a leaking tap forming stalagmites around the darkening maw of my consciousness, but each time I sit at the mouth of the cave I find myself taking in its natural beauty and breathing a little deeper. The last time I step out of my psychiatrist's office the clock by her computer is exactly five minutes fast and each tick between each tock of each clock lasts a whole second.

path to recovery

Red brick houses hide behind
lashes of ivy, or perhaps
a tree blossoming in season,
scattering pollen on the wind.

Uneven asphalt winds its way
around the duck, goose, moorhen pond
with the wrought iron bench
covered in graffiti

and an old man with a bag of peas.
I remember the storm
that hit the tree so hard it broke
into a thousand matchsticks,

raining splinters on the climbing frames
usually adorned with a thousand birds.
Uncut grass ripples in the wind
like ocean waves

or maybe, sometimes, it sits in bunches
under the summer sun
when it's been dry enough to permit
the council worker and their grass cutter.

The path slopes down and
threatens to slippen after rain
churns the mud and leaves to mulch
and the canopy keeps away the sun,

keeping everything in shadow
as far as the so-called river,
ankle deep in a brickwork gutter
matching the houses nearby.

We'll be here soon enough, polished stone
adorned with flowers, balloons, grief,
with a thousand birds,
a thousand matchsticks,

but today the gates are open.
I wonder how many Victorian graves
worked at the Victorian mill
where I now sit opposite a therapist

in a painfully clean, white room
in a semi-comfortable chair
to talk about birds
and matchsticks.

chalk

Cats curled up inches from his face
copying him on the guest bed
with the duvet swirling around
his foetal body like a galaxy.
Wind and rain
batter the window pane
and he can't help but think
it's the same in his brain.

He started eating chalk
to see if it could rewrite his mind
and how it's aligned,
only to find
it's been far from kind
so he's there, entwined
in the bedsheets and been left behind,
confined to the storm,
wondering if chalk can outlast the rain.

pillars of creation

do not strive to be so hard upon yourself that you throw
your gaze onto a render of us with misplaced awe

you are already who we are; our dust meets yours
we coalesce at the Heart of All and find our own journeys
through the Arteries of Everything in such a way that
connection will always be in our deepest roots

we see you, we saw you,
we know what you were and who you are
because we are the same
there is little need to wonder of our greatness
when you have given rise so much of your own

do not strive to be so hard upon yourself that you throw
your gaze onto a render of us with misplaced awe

feel like neither a snap nor a wink
despite however much the feeling of such
can drive the ashes further into your lungs
and your eyes further away from your self

nothing is permanent
we are not permanent
we are already scattered on the solar winds
waiting for when the time is right
waiting for our dust to meet

stepping out

    i.

the seed of worry, unnoticed, allowed to propagate
for half a life, taking half a life, leaving only
half a life to be lived. Shackles of uncertainty
grip tighter and bruise my wrists, ankles, throat,

ego, with every unmade act until I believe my
own lie that purple is the colour of my skin
and I wonder why I'm the only person with
galaxies imprinted around my farthest reaches

    ii.

enough is enough, I decide. Is decided for me. I
talk to a stranger, I swallow tablets, I melt along
the lines of a canal to drown constellations, and
scrub at the stars to make the lights go out. It's

thankless and I don't know if I have the strength,
the fortitude, the desire to keep building a ladder
where each new rung I'm yet to climb above me
is taken from an old one supporting me below

iii.

soon I find myself floating in the cosmos as it fades around me, what I am fades around me, what I know fades around me. My purple skin turns pinker and doesn't scream to the touch

of cheap aluminium-plated brass holding on like a scared child. The shackles are gone but when I take a closer look I see that the stars surrounding me are falling flakes of metal

iv.

a fine film of guilt coats me all over. The shackles are gone and I am granted the movement I have been starved of in my half-life, but for the price of binding the world to my own needs, moving

the restraints instead of releasing them. I feel good that my lack of freedom frees me in a way I didn't think possible. I look to the sky and see galaxies swirling over head. It's easier. I'm happy.

v.

dusk lasts day after day, the sun hangs heavy
in the sky, an eternal sunset I'm happy to
watch at the expense of a new dawn,
at the expense of starting over, at the expense

of everyone else. Days pass to months and the
sky slowly bruises itself into submission. I don't
want it to turn blue again but the purple blackens
tightly around my throat. I can taste the stars.

vi.

my eyes are forced open by the sound of life
interrupting where it has no business. The
stars have gone from the clear blue sky, they
have made their way back to my farthest reaches

 but they are fainter and the metal doesn't
scratch the bottom of my tongue like it used
to. The chains are quieter and each step adds
another link, each step makes the next easier.

i'm sorry, stephen

Whenever I went to your flat you would be, without fail, sat in that deep chair with your knees under your chin, while a breeze came in from the narrow gap of the open window, lazily unspooling the string of smoke from the end of the king-sized cigarette you'd rolled out into the November cold. I'd try not to choke on the cloud of smoke but it would hit the back of my throat, mixed with the many aromatic notes of lavender and citrus, vanilla and eucalyptus from candles and incense sticks and nearly make me sick, but I loved the way it filled my nose and how I'd carry you home on my clothes. I'm ashamed to say I took it as an easy way out, an excuse to evade the tough conversation I wasn't mature enough to sit down and have. You could see something had changed and even let me go and put my thoughts in writing because it would be easier than biting my tongue with my head on your lap while I stared at the floor. Your building was on the main road and in the months that followed I'd drive past every Sunday, twice, as I made my way to and from work. I'd look at your window not sure what I was hoping for, but trying to catch a glance all the same through my hypocritical shame like a lost lamb in the congregation hoping to be saved from damnation. It would be nice to think adding ten candles to my cake since I sorely mishandled the situation meant I would be a better person, but here I am putting a letter in a bottle and throwing it out to sea instead of speaking to you directly.

sandwich board

it was too big when I was younger
my knees knocked against it
and my shins banged against the bottom edge
and the chains would rattle and swing wildly
and my forearms would hang limply out each side

people would look at it instead of me but
sometimes it was nice to have a shell to hide inside

I grew so the board fits my proportions more
but still I catch my wrists on the chains and
my knees knock where my shins once chafed
and as hard as I look down I can never see
what's on it, even though that's where
everyone still looks when they look at me
because they think it tells them who I am

summer evenings on public transport

A suffocating day in July
the kind that pulls the air from your
lungs with vigour
and puts it back begrudgingly
with a sluggish fist

the kind where darkness doesn't exist
and your skin is mottled and damp
from before you had the chance
to take your first breath
until long after your last

the kind where you find the unwanted
taste of other people
sticking to your palate like cement
that shows no signs of drying,
where surreptitiously picking sand
from between your teeth
makes each grain chafe your dry
tongue
down to a spike

the kind that, in your touch-starved haze,
in the liminal space closed off from
a drunken sky too shy for darkness,
electricity sparks where bare skin
spills out
like God
reaching for Adam
giving life

the man with a lance in his chest

There's a man I've seen around town
he's got a lance sticking out of his chest.

He looks like that old TV ad
where we're meant to marvel at the fountain pen
going through the tin can as if that's a feature
you want from your writing utensil.

It's a deep scarlet colour and juts out of his concave sternum
but he walks around like he doesn't see it,
maybe it's the same as the way our brain tricks us
into not seeing our nose.

One time I asked why he doesn't take it out,
make his life a lot easier, and he told me
it's the lance that keeps him alive,
that while pulling it out would make life easier
for him and everyone around him
it would only be a short while until all of him
leaked from the hole.

With his fingers already tight around the handle
he asked if I thought inconvenience was enough of a reason
to watch him drain away. I pleaded with him to let go,
but he misunderstood and pulled.

The lance showed no signs of ending,
like a magician's string of handkerchiefs,
until finally the prong emerged
tugging at the skin
removing a knife from tar, as though his body tried to hold on
as long as it could before admitting defeat and falling back
into its proper shape.

I still see him around town,
the scarlet lance pulled all his colour with it.

He says he's happy not standing out,
not getting stuck in doorways,
but his mouth and his eyes haven't got their story straight.

a bouquet for alan in lieu of being able to do anything meaningful

I only met him the once,
we sat together on a park bench,
but still I felt compelled to leave
something for him.

We start with a bed of dead leaves,
pulling sadness out of the earth
with its oranges, browns and dark greens
dappled with black mulch patches

all accompanied by fronds of weeping willow
curling around the edges of the bouquet
like fingers, like a veil, like a curtain
trying to close over the

dashes of colour marigolds and harebells offer
through the leaves, as if to call out
the futility of burying grief.

A stalk or two of American cudweed
and pheasant's eye get added to the mix,
bringing an unforgettable
texture to a watchful, reverent eye

while a single sprig of lilac wilts
next to a pink and white carnation,
exuding disappointment at the thought
of wasted genius.

A cluster of zinnia burns like a
sunset sliding slowly out of sight,
so we keep the petals in the middle,
bold and unmissable,
a reminder of its absence.

The arrangement is cumbersome and
I'm ashamed to admit
even though I've passed down the street
several times
I haven't brought myself to
revisit the memorial and deliver it.

oh, romeo

crane your neck a little less
have the pedestal be the
bitterest thing you swallow before
it's too late to undo
the folly of excitable youth.

what you deserve

The problem with going to bed happy
at night is that my brain won't allow it.
You're not allowed to be happy, it says,
and asking why is the worst thing I could do
but I do it every time like a moth to a flame and
suddenly I'm flicking through a stack of receipts
that make me a Terrible Human Being even
though I've worked hard at not being
That Person anymore.

I foolishly took it to heart when Chbosky said
we accept the love we think we deserve,
spending my life being wrong about what I
thought love owed me.
It took a long time to believe the man I loved
loved me back and even longer to admit
I deserved it. But sometimes, still, the night closes
around me like clasped hands squeezing a sponge
free of all its water, incapable of pushing back.

body swap secrets

The boy looked up at the deer and the deer looked down at the boy.

Shallow water rippled outward from their feet and extended forever in all directions, reflecting the stars and constellations of the night sky the boy never thought to learn the names of.

"Well?" the boy asked stubbornly. He scowled so deep his eyebrows almost met the tip of his nose. His hands dug firmly into his hips and his feet were planted in place. Despite the water lapping at his shoes, his socks and feet remained dry.

The deer sighed a heavy sigh and walked closer to the boy. With each silent step, its infinite fractal antlers shimmered with galaxies. The deer bowed and pressed its forehead gently against the boy's, whose scowl quickly gave way to tears.

Through his cries of anguish the boy wrapped his arms around the deer's jaw and sobbed into its fur. When the boy felt as though there were no tears left in him the deer withdrew, as if it knew the boy's feelings and understood his catharsis.

"You grieve because you have lost something you love," the deer said without moving its mouth. It spoke with the voice of the boy's father. Or as much as the boy could remember such a distant sound.

"I know," the boy responded, wiping the remaining tears from his face with his slight, bony wrist. "I need the secret to making it stop."

"My son," the deer said with a softness from a perspective on eternity, "there is no secret to grief, no method to make it relent."

The boy didn't like this answer but held his tongue. His shoulders sank in defeat as the tang of copper fizzed at the back of his throat.

The deer, seeing this reaction, took pity and continued, "Grief sits in the chair once occupied by Love. To dine with Grief is to dine with Love and to know the one you lost is still with you."

The boy remained quiet and held out his hand. The deer repeated its bow and let the boy lay his palm on its forehead. Tears welled again in the boy's eyes and caught the starlight, refracting rainbows around the edges of his vision. As he cried silently into the water, two great white antlers grew from his head.

fertiliser

the hand that pulls the line

I've spent the day entirely out of body,
a little to the left, I like to call it, because it feels
like I've been detached and am slightly out of sync
with everything, including myself.

The reception in my brain is static. Fog. It's trying
to walk through treacle or running in a dream.
There's no traction. My limbs feel tense but absent
at the same time. I'm paralysed.

I'm adrift in the void, the pressure of nothingness
choking, squeezing, constricting, suffocating.
I want to claw at my throat and my temples to let the
pressure but I'm a little to the left.

Your fingers lock with mine and I am
breathing again, thinking again, finding my way back
into my body again, pulled back in line
by a rope knotted just right

brid

My granddad would drive
with his one eye
and his sluggish left side
to the same car park by
the train station every time.

We'd make our way
to the beach at a leisurely pace.
Sometimes we'd stop for cakes
at the Boyes cafe
but sometimes we'd wait
to get ice cream later.

Down on the promenade we'd go
at a speed befitting old
people until we got to the big slope
where we'd stop and get chips and hold
them out of reach of the seagulls watching close.

We'd take in the view
while we finished our food
and sometimes we'd look for a new
piece of hideous kitschy art like eyes glued
to stones and shells that wouldn't suit
any place in any room.

Annie's truck sold waffles and ice cream
further down the south beach
so we'd pull up some seats
and look out over the marina while we'd eat.
After we finished we'd
head back the way we came on tired feet.

We'd stop one last time
in the penny arcades
and try to win cheap tat to bring home.
The water was never blue
but then neither were we.

a certain summer

August, you are mine.
August, the colour of blue and peach and orange.
The pastel month, August.
Daylight hours stretch across August and meet at each end.
August, with its habit of having nothing but evenings.
The sky is bruised with the wrong crayons in August.
Feeling balanced in the middle,
                              ignoring that August is tipping you over.
August, peering through your curtains without you asking.
August, knocking on your door and stepping inside
                                            as soon as you open it.
August, locking its fingers with yours and pulling you
                                            into the cloudless sky.
The warm August caress making your hair stand on end.
Goosebumps call for August to kiss them down, one by one.
August flies in through the open window.
The ruffled bed sheets wait for August in the heavy, still air.
One hand takes another and traces circles on a palm
                                            as August opens wide.

August, you are mine.

no more gruel

drink it in
taste the fresh sights and sounds against your virgin lips
a cool cocktail filled with flavours you never knew
in all your years clinging to the North Sea with itchy fingers
pretending not to clutch pursed mouth or
enjoy the allure of apple

grow plump with plenty
fill out your hollowed cheeks and your inward chest
a sponge soaking up the life it was late to start living
colour after colour seeping into its skin

have your fill in a feast with friends
let them feed you until you've learnt your own recipes
to return the favour under a string of fairy lights
on a bench in a beer garden surrounded by ivy
and concrete and everything you ever wanted

cut me open

Cut me open and find lavender,
hydrangea and tangles of ivy

Cut me open for branches
of a fern bush that
are pulled out in bunches
leaving spring clinging
to your fingertips

Cut me open and release boats
of gravy, thick like tar
with an onion sting that
tickles the back of your throat
before you've even started to pour

Cut me open for Sunday Roast
Monday Roast
As Many Days As Possible Roast

Cut me open and see time pass
like rings in a tree stump
hardening its edges each year
and forcing through
to grow again

Cut me open and see arms
wrapped around me, fingers
linked like chains, like zips
holding things close to
bursting seams, always touching
always contact
always a unit

Cut me open and hear laughter
cascade like a waterfall
bouncing over rocks and folding
over, making more of itself
amplifying its sound
through flora and fauna
through life itself
spreading life
giving life

Cut me open and see how much life I give

Cut me open and know
I am loved.

soundtrack to a life: a certain trigger

I sleep with my hands across my chest and
waking up I need a lift.
My heart is always racing,
hold me now 'til my breath runs out
I just want to feel comfortable.
One in a million,
someone better than myself
inside your head are things I never thought about.
Your eyes are big when they're so close
I can't remember why I started hurting
I've been waiting to forget.
Close your eyes if you're scared
I prefer to keep my eyes wide open

in and out

I feel each grain of sand against my heels
the balls of my feet
between each of my toes

I know that when I leave all the
coarseness will be gone
leaving all of me smooth and new

waves whisper against the shore
caressing the edge of the land
like the soft head of a cat

calling out in a hushed voice
calming my mind to oscillate in time
with each gentle stroke

the waves don't wash back out to sea
I watch as each one gets closer
then fades into the sand leaving a stain

on the surface it looks as though it's gone
but the water is making its way deep
to hold the sand together

dance, darling

It's getting dark in July
but I am not tired yet. I sit and watch
her from a distance as she, dressed in innocence,
twirls on the floor hand-in-hand with
everyone who helped her get here.

It's late but I am not tired yet.
For the first time in years I am not tired.
After an age of
weary dogs gnawing on my bones
for their only sustenance
I am not tired.

We claim to not be children anymore but
under these lights,
under these stained-glass substitutes
that pull me back effortlessly to the time of the
primary school disco, I am drowned
by the revelation we could
never be anything else.

I am nine years old on the floor
beside her bed – our recording
studio – reading along with the latest offerings
from the Smash Hits CD lyric book
while we record the songs
over whatever used to be on
old cassette tapes, and try to keep
out the hum of the boiler during our DJ patter.

She is in charge of the
clunky buttons my inexperienced
fingers haven't yet got the hang
of, pressing play and record
at the same time with the deftness of
someone whose age has reached
double digits,
practically an adult.
We capture our lives on ribbon
we think will last
forever
because we haven't given anything
the chance to come along
and tell us otherwise.

It is dark in July
but I am not tired yet. The songs from our
ribbons are here and she is twirling
along in kind and makes me
believe maybe things can be
forever as long as we let them.

I keep my distance to take
in the mise-en-scene
of the moment,
savour the red wine day
at the back of my throat.
As I sit and hold the bouquet
my knuckles are white
around the seat of my chair
because the moment I let go
I'm going to take flight.

off-balance

Life billows from my head like ink in water
one of those undersea thermal vents,
an old chimney stack before the factory was abandoned.
I am heavy in my weightlessness as
pins prick holes in the parachute of my peripheral
and I am about to freefall under a tattered rag

My grasp gives me nothing with my fingers,
a clumsy pincer at the edge of the fray,
missing its mark as I battle with the
unsteady deck of the rocking ship.
I need to find my feet.

Again I close my fingers around nothing
instead of the something I was going for as the
storm on the ocean picks up and makes my
heavy head fall to the side and sets the world an angle.
Clutching the side of the ship I whimper
weakly and try to steady myself, but the frayed
edges burn away more and more of my vision.
I need to find my feet.
I need to find my feet.
I can't find my feet.
I can't find my eyes, my lungs, my ears.

A hand moves in front of me, my hand,
shifting into my line of sight that blooms and spreads
like a blot of ink falling onto paper
and I learn that solid ground came up
to greet me at an acute angle.

And then there's you,
softly burrowing into the centre of each sense
pulling the world in with you to help me understand it,
a calmness in your voice that I know is hiding a storm
comes to me like an angelic chorus and even though
you're behind me I can feel you unclench, release tension,
as I come back to you the third time you ask.

Upside down, we wait for dawn inside cotton cocoons
taking caterpillar bites from slices of bread,
you join me in the undergrowth
at the edge of the forest assessing the damage,
calculating the rebuild effort.

I find myself behind your eyes throughout the day
and watch as I splinter like timber crashing into the marsh,
throw shadow and sludge all over your face
for you to wipe away before it dries and seals you shut.

Later that evening you are drawn upstairs
by the sound of me crying in the shower, crushed
beneath the weight of everything landing on top of me.
You take all the pieces and push them back into place.
I can find my feet.

dinosaur skeleton

Old sepia photographs, stained and
frayed at the edges, where the people
had to wait an age for the process to
be complete, show sullen faces
lacking enjoyment and we blow that
into a macrocosm of a joyless age.

We forget the past was in full colour
with smiles and tears and solemnity
alike, and as life's conveyor belt takes
us out of view we're left to create a
jigsaw without even being aware
we are missing most of the pieces.

Our footprints will last more than any
who have walked before us, but my
trail cannot tell you what I was
wearing, or what I was feeling, or what
I was carrying, only the path I took
and whether or not I was alone.

The image will always be incomplete
like too little skin stretched too thinly
over too much bone, or a photograph
that takes so long to complete that
smiling would put your face in agony
so instead you sit, stoic, at ease.

I have no control over how I will be
reconstructed, even words written on
a page capture but a fleeting moment
in time, a view seen only in passing on
the conveyor, a reconstitution of me
wouldn't – couldn't – be truly faithful.

Look less at the bones you're set to
leave behind. Resist the temptation to
carve open your flesh and see what
will be left for others because we're
nothing more than old photographs
retrofitted into a macrocosm.

generation game, family fortunes et al.

At the heart of the burgundy pebble-dashed house in the middle of the terrace, the studio audience sits filled with food and drink and love, a fullness that keeps you warm in November, the *nice to see you to see you nice* kind brought on by being squashed onto one sofa answering *what a hot spot's not*. Part of the generation who never knew Cilla Black as a singer, too young to understand the nuances of *Blind Date* but able to enjoy the theme tune, when the dates were hilariously tragic and hearing the line *before you decide, here's our Graham* in that melodic Scouse accent. Wondering where these hundred people were found to sound that unforgettable klaxon when *our survey says* you couldn't decipher their guesses correctly, and every week, without fail, the only thing I could remember on that conveyor belt was the cuddly toy because of how wild the audience went for it. *It's only easy if you know it* was the soundtrack to our weekends as the studio audience of six was convinced we could make it to the million without even needing the lifelines and wondering if we'd be anyone's choice if they used theirs. Losing your spot on the sofa when someone uses the clever ploy to ask for a cuppa, but the answer to *say what you see* is always Embodiment of Happiness which Mr. Chips might have a hard time replicating but we manage to do it every weekend without fail. My back rests against the sofa, possibly a pair of shins. Someone's hand runs through my hair that only stops to cross fingers, in a prayer to the lottery idol after its prophet Mystic Meg peered into her crystal ball and miraculously described everyone sitting in every living room. Crossed fingers radiate the mantra *it could be you* and while it would be nice, it was the source of lacking any religious or spiritual fulfilment. I knew it never would be us, but as such an unburdened child I never felt I needed it. *Let's have a look at what you could have won!* No need, Jim, I've got it right here.

standing in the filth

Skin peels away like damp, rotten bark
exposing the fresh pink wood underneath,
raw to the wind and rain and sun
ready to harden into a new layer.

Leaves turn brown and curl at the edges like
soap dishes to trap the run-off until
it sits so long the leaves grow heavy and
sodden and fall from their grace, leaving
branches bare, exposing thoughts and feelings
until the season ends and green returns.

Everything falls down to the dirt.
Everything becomes the dirt.
The bark, the leaves, the skin, the self.
Take all the rot and push it down,
stand in the compost,
grow fresh and new.

what's yours is mine

It's one of those things that goes
unnoticed for a while, picking
up steam as a relationship grows,
more and more spaghetti sticking

to the wall as we sling our tongues
from the pan, more and more
paint pouring from our lungs
and mixing into a new colour on the floor

The way you move and the words you use
find their way into my routine
like some Ancient Greek muse,
just as I can be seen,

like moss, covering you.
We make more than a language of our own,
we make a world for just the two
of us to flourish in alone.

made from trees

We grew up surrounded by trees
where each one gave a branch to who we became.
We grew up surrounded by trees
that grew with us and lifted our names
in their knots and notches,
they watched us with kindness
and each one gave a branch to who we became.
More often than not you could find us
under the dapple hunting for dock leaves
that we would eagerly show to our parents as
they watched us with kindness
under the dapple hunting for dock leaves
and thistles and weeds that stuck to our clothes.
Memory comes to me in shades of green,
deep riches from before we were beset by thieves
who took everything we had ever been,
filling their pockets with what they thought they were owed
and never questioned our worth.
Nostalgia comes to me in shades of green
and brown and smells strongly of
petrichor and how we used to play in damp earth.
We grew up surrounded by trees
under the dapple hunting for dock leaves
and never once questioned our worth.

...and flow

I am here, slowly eroding away on an empty beach,
where only a wish can carry me out,
keep up with what I what I want to achieve for
my world. The sand shifts in ways that I can't.
When all form is taken away from the hem of
the stitching of the cliffs at my back,
promises of what could be possible tug
where unseen fingers unravel the town until empty,
sway in the wind over the edge of the world,
thread after thread after thread
capable of changing anything. More often than not
a stone sits in the centre of an empty room, in
my mind, in place of my thoughts. White noise
of the waves coming up to meet me overtakes
the overwhelming and seemingly endless crashing
of the contents rolling around inside my head,
giving me a small window to try and grasp any
chance to be calm, with it only
constricting. Openness makes me lose that fleeting
call to bind my wrists and ankles within
the cinder blocks beneath me in the sand
and I return to thoughts I can call my own
despite the whispers in my ear.
There is nothing stretching out into the dark,
my own way lies in my future, I can see
into the open expanse. I am standing in
ankle-deep potential – the furthest I'll ever go
threatens to remain unknown, a static life on
the edge of the shore where the hard line
burns my chest. I weave towards

the lightless and indiscernible horizon.
From the precipice of shadow
the maelstrom fills my lungs and
makes the hairs on my arms stand on end.
Another world sits on the other side
against the line that ebbs and flows at my feet,
twists and breaks with electric uncertainty.
Held close, I watch as piece by piece
I am pulled in surrounded by everything I ever
achieved. With arms open wide
to show me the unknown possibilities I could have,
the vast expanse begs I take its proffered hand.

painting glass jars

We sit downstairs in a gay bar, the first one I've been inside in nearly a decade, surrounded by our ilk on chairs too high for all of us, but we sit comfortably both in them and in ourselves without the need to leave a piece at the door. Glass jars sit under the lights, throwing sunbursts onto tables in a strange act of irony as though they know their future. We each take a blank canvas ready to stick ourselves to its sides but minds just as blank draw from nothing to draw nothing.

What is there to say? I begin with the intentions of honouring a lost generation but I find myself clutching the paint marker and thinking only empty platitudes. The colours feel too vivid for remembrance, painting a wild thing of beauty feels a disservice to those who weren't allowed to be that way in life, though some might argue the merits of offering that in death. Eventually I take a muted colour and begin placing dots around the jar, leaving plenty of open space so when the candle is inside it'll throw an inverted night sky across everything it touches. There's an obligation to draw the ribbon. The red pen will be replaced before the evening is over.

A photograph sits at the front of my mind. It's a photo of the San Francisco Gay Men's Chorus taken in the early nineties, with those who survived facing the camera in white. Seven stars in a sky of black backs turned for each person lost. The next jar I take is so meticulously coated in darkness, no light can get through. As I turn the canvas my fingertips turn grey like old bruises. Caught by the still-wet paint they mar the precise texture like a man attempting to sweep away his own footprints. I leave seven squares unpainted in a pattern that almost takes the shape of the Plough. After waiting for the black to dry I repeat the process of staining my fingers all over again. Once finished, the light of the candle inside will be dimmed for each light snuffed out too soon, a fading community rebuilding from the ground up, but I realise in my reverence I've given them the same hand they were dealt when they were alive by hiding their light. I understand why the table is filled with colours.

Taking my final jar and the brightest pens, the bones of stained glass stretch out across the glass like root network, like a delta system, like clay hardening in a kiln. Then the spaces between the bones fill with colour, creating a stained mosaic of rainbow hands holding rainbow hand, embracing each other in the safety and sanctuary of a painted glass jar.

chalk part II

Chalk swings on the pendulum of permanence,
sits comfortably in the crook of my hand
like an old friend, a friend I betray and erode
each time I take it in my hand and scribe
false satisfaction with temporary lines that have faded
when the next morning comes and I return
with the intention of wearing it down yet again.

Every day I sit before the board,
read its faded words as though they were
sent from some higher being telling me

what I want to hear
what I need to know
a message from the divine delivering
absolution on a haloed promise.

To remember the mantra I take out the chalk,
sacrifice the integrity of a friend for
personal gain as I trace over the lines left for me.

yumbo

warthog approaches the watering hole
in a world where pigs are pretty

tusk and tuft, welcome traits
after hurriedly drinking
just enough and fleeing from predators
whose arrival is inevitable

now warthog sits and takes his time
savours the freshness of the water pouring
down his throat
dripping from his chin

water is plentiful
pigs are pretty

sonnet of gentle reflections

The rustling grass and ripples on the lake
give sight and sound to nature's gentle soul,
a living, breathing mother. Give control
to her, be not afraid to let her take
your hand and soothe the storm you often find
enraged inside yourself, 'til all that's left
is soft around the edges and bereft
of all unwanted things that make your kind,
adoring heart a heavy stone to weigh.
As water holds reflections of the sky
so, too, our selves reflect and amplify
surroundings that we spend our time. So may
      the place the mirror of our heart finds rest
      bestow on us reflections to be blessed.

soundtrack to a life: high as hope

Hold on to each other
and let the river rush in,
let it slide down to the sea.
Hold me down,
you can always find me here.
You remind me that it's such a wonderful thing to love
because you loved me the most.
For a moment we were able to be still
and for a moment I forget to worry.

                                    What else could be better than this?

mother

Propagations propagate,
make their way into new homes
with windowsills
never patched
forever drenched in sun light.

Spilling out of terracotta,
a limb of ivy has no
idea where it needs to go,
but instinctively finds its way
without thinking,
without questioning.
Everything comes back around,
hand in recursive hand.

Can a windowsill be too big
yet not big enough
in the same breath?
The same breath that plays
in reverse to give
what it can,
reciprocating nurture
as second nature.

An estuary of light
flows through patchwork glass
where brackish time
courts caddish tide
from this
to the next
until over the end.

Nobody saw how it happened
but a new plant hangs
out the window
into the place time and tide
kept secret under the soil.

It breathes its second nature
beyond the confines of comfort,
stretching the fibres of its
stem until it splits and
knits itself back together
into a structure more
capable of support.
It breathes with a confidence
believing the nature of
what sits further away than the soil
that clings to its roots
finds solace in reciprocation.

close your eyes and think of flåm

the bustling town centre
is made up of a lodge, an
    indoor market, a convenience

store and a couple of
eateries, the boat we
    disembark is the biggest

thing here by orders of
magnitude and stepping
    onto the emerald

grass sends pulses of
calm through my body
    up from my feet

through my fingertips. All
around us is a wall of
    green rock reaching

so high it disappears
into the clouds, I'm sitting
    in the palm of a giant

    who's whispering into my
ear that everything is going
        to be okay. Waterfalls drip

    through the cracks of her
fingers and spread a fine
        mist about the area that

    brings a freshness I've
never before experienced. The
        buildings sitting in the lines

    of her palm stand out
against the green with their
        yellows and reds. I have

    never known a place be so
quiet in all my life. From
        the heart line we fill a

    basket with sweets and crisps
that have Norwegian names
        we can't pronounce and

      the sun line offers a pair
of gloves even though
          it's August because it'll

      be winter eventually
and these are the warmest
          things I've ever put on

      my hands. An old steam
train traces the edge of the
          fjord, the giant raises me

      higher and higher
until I'm close enough to
          thank God and it feels

      like the sole purpose
of the journey as I
          descend back through the

      weather-beaten houses
and black church with a
          peace that I couldn't have

ever guessed existed. She
holds me close again
    and I fall into her head

    line for a lemonade, lamenting
the fact I know when her
    fate line sends us on our

    way she will never hold me
again. She cries as our
    boat turns around in the

    bay, we watch the grey
unfurl and desaturate the
    world around us, we watch

    the clouds burst as they
mourn our passing. I
    stand at the rear of the

    boat until the land has
gone completely from
    view and I know this

    place, this soft cradle, will
one day come back to
    be my life line.

sleeping lessons part II

I put my arm around him and the noise stops
like a draught excluder keeping the whistle
away from the bottom of a door

The things I needed to do, the voices I
needed to drown, gone, forgotten,
as I listen to him breathing next to me.

iron man 3: a christmas film released in april

This is what I came here for.
I ascend Angel's gate into the arms of
haloed lamp lights that cradle my stigmat-
ism, as if making it all the way up the concrete
altar is some sort of holy rite. Shivers greet
me in tepid spring, my knuckles lose their
bones and keep from sprouting olive branches
over vast seas turned inside-out from endless
nameless storms. There is power held in names,
power held in knowing those names, power I want
to yield for the strength in my branches but don't
know how. Overwhelming every strand of me is the
feeling I shouldn't be here, the feeling I am standing
where others get to stand and I am taking up someone
else's space, but his branches braved those nameless storms
to entwine with mine and bridge more gaps than I knew I had.
We stay close and let floods pass by that don't recognise
the damage they left below the water line or how many nails
softened by saline tides still stick out from algae- coated
cobblestones, left to turn yellow – the colour of
forgetfulness – so I turn to warmer light and cling to the
growing patches of dry land under sunset beams.
This is where I'm supposed to be.
Two feet firmly rooted in the wild grasses
promised by paradise, bones and branches making
themselves known to one another in a place
where shame hasn't been given a name and
therefore holds no power over me.

autumn brings the ghosts

this year it happened earlier than usual so I was
caught off guard when the first leaf rusted from its
branch and landed at my feet. I finally
took the moment to look around me and saw this
was, in fact, far from the first – the streets were
lined with copper, and branches reached out with
gnarled fingers to pick up their loose change
but once the coin is in the fountain the wish won't
come true if you take it back out again.

there's a freshness to the air. Not quite the
minty glacial freshness of winter that cuts through
your lungs but a warmer freshness like pulling
bedding off the radiator and wrapping it
around yourself. The smell of leaves turning to mulch
offer opportunity in the form of
pennies sticking to the back of the throat.

my childhood turns and looks at me with wide eyes
and asks what I'm doing. He's not accusatory,
he's inquisitive, but I know whatever he has on his
busy schedule is better than what I've
got going on so when I ask he leads me by
the hand to play with plastic dinosaurs made from
refined versions of their past selves
and die cast Hot Wheels cars because he still
lives in a world where they can exist side by side
along with anything else he can imagine.

outside the window, leaves parachute to the
ground in a blizzard of earth tones. My childhood
is too engrossed in making a pterodactyl
swoop down and pick up a limousine to notice and
when I want to show him the sight I realise the
boy is not me, he is not my ghost. He is my
blood. I had not been clinging to the past like I
thought but unfolding the future. The brass
coating the floor doesn't mean the end of anything
as much as it means the start of
something else. It means neither. It
means both. A cycle greater than what I could
ever expect to comprehend so I may as
well sit under the collapsing canopy and play
with toys that stretch across lifetimes.

bicep stain

sunrise creeps up green against glass
colliding with the sunset – deep and purple,
still fluttering from lungs, through lips –
brushing everything with white noise

Conifers blur into the cracks of concrete,
my eyes stretch them into string theory
between blossoming worlds brought into
existence by the pressures of nebulae
retreating to the curves of lullaby walls

Patchwork fields
over tendons
into strands
under water

Flooding plains soaking down to the marrow
my body makes more of me
inspired by the parts of you that took root
pollinating in the crosswind that –
even under the ocean –
spreads and grows in soil tilled by the tongue
refusing to fall from our own

My head leans into yours and hopes
when it pulls away
more of you will cling to me

cheap waltzers

Breathe.
Breathe long and deep.
Circles dance around the edges of more circles
fractals working down fractures
cutting through the baseline of creation
until the canvas smears out of focus and burns
across the insides of my eyelids.
Dreamless nights push me down through feathered
hands, sifting neon and ultraviolet into sand and sea
rippling around my knuckles, and when the morning
greets me I am heavy in its arms. Worlds birthed around me
pool at my ankles and pinch with a breathlessness
only afforded to Achilles himself, where the air
fills my lungs instead of swirling them around and
finally I know what it means to breathe.

555

two ferns
joined at the soul

roots weaving through
the same soil

leaves entwined
so only the stems
can tell who's who

next to one another
over
under

sand and water
turn to concrete

left to sit
in a
wooden mould
with flowers
tangled in the cracks
gold spun into
fabric
chlorophyll
arteries
souls

beaming a shining
richness from
pockets and leaves

bettering modesty
and learning
how to show pride

a cornucopia floats
upstream on a
thick river

handing seeds and
leaves to every
other child along
the bank

for them to
plant in the ground

nurture a
bountiful feast
of their own some
day

prisms dance
along the horizon
with soft
allure and
sure footing

to wrap refractions
of light against
their own
reflections

to look back
at each other
at itself

to hold something
to show a love
hard fought for
and long denied
climbing more
with each new round

pulling further
further
further
splitting at the seams
pouring with pearls
but never
overburdened

as above
no more below

water flows into
a ravine
the wind reminisces
and catches
each drop like

a mother who
thinks
she knows what's
best for her
child

pulls the water
close to her
chest and
spirits away to
gods know where

so while the top
lays verdant
and fertile

the floor below
is barren
empty
hollow
silent

nothing stirs
in the rough
terrain until the
sky catches
fire and
douses itself out
for the new shoots
of life
to push through
dust and rock

reach for the moon
an older friend
from a previous
life
too out of reach
to nurture
growth
so as it drops
below the
horizon
the new shoots
follow
their old friend
and go
back to the dirt

each morning
the sun
climbs from
its duvet
greeted
by empty land

despite knowing
despite remembering
something used
to be there
waiting for
it to rise
that time is over

the age of the sun
lost to those
who supped from
the morning
given way
to the era of
the moon
to the era of

How It Was Before

and we are
left without
warmth
except for what
we make ourselves
by holding close
in the time
we have

it's never really night time

Two inches of snow and I can read the pages
of a book under the hum of midnight.
Those who shy away when the night arrives stay
bold and hold it back. When timelines are scratched
into exercise books, the blot of the Tyrannosaurus-Rex
sits closer to smudges of moon landings and Ice Bucket
Challenge videos than it does to the mark of the
Stegosaurus. Even when we are gone we are sardines
pressed close, everything we have ever conceived
thrown into a tight space. We are still together.
Cowboys and samurai walked the streets with pirates
and Jack the Ripper. Reflections keep the stars
a mystery – such ancient ingénue are not welcome
amongst the youth of dinosaurs.

If I wanted to, I could close my eyes and feel my atoms
fizzle out, stretch me out from the big bang to the
heat death of everything, nothing but night on either side.

If I wanted to.

soundtrack to a life: wall of arms

The worms are what await me.
That's what they're singing in the shadows
where weaker hearts have made a home.
With all the strength of
empty hands and tired eyes
those thoughts are behind me
and the thought of you, it was crystal clear.
The four letter word that you found
showing us the way,
growing old together
healed without scab or scar.

the living building

Still reeling from the open wounds carved into
me by Theseus when he left me for dead,
I find myself in an old Japanese tea house
sitting alone on the hillside in an act of solidarity

When I try to remember entering the place
my mind draws a blank, but I can see
vividly the image of its dark wooden roof
surrounded by pale cherry blossoms,
a bold egg in a gentle nest
enclosed around a soul with an irregular
beat, waiting for the gestation
forming with what came before

For five hundred years, the tea house has nestled
comfortably in the hillside making the same
concoctions, recipes unchanged for centuries
for each person who left their
shoes and their baggage in the hall.

Tea has never drawn me in,
making me a bad Northerner and giving
me a complex to be discussed at another time,
but I am enamoured by the old man
sitting opposite me as he pours from a teapot
filled with impossibly coloured hibiscus petals

Intuitively he knows what is eating away at me
even though I don't realise this at first when he
directed my attention to the beams above our heads
to the boards beneath our feet
at the petals in my cup

None of these things held the centuries in their grains
they were merely the components bearing the torches
in the time allotted for me to offer my appreciation
here and now, each drop of rain absorbed into
the pavement as quickly as it passes our eyes
following the thousands of drops that came before
to be followed by thousands more, all part of one storm

The essence is the truth.
Endless rain falls and the storm has the same name
beams of wood sit side by side and birth a tea house
lasting beyond their decay, and with every plank
replaced the name of the tea house
stays the same above the door
a little more sure each time it's repainted

The teacup warms my hands
my sinuses clear when I inhale the rainbow steam
there's a sweetness to the tea that knits the edges of my
wounds together, a little more sure of what's beneath

make sculptures

I welcome

myself

in
my current state,
forming
enjoyment

from within.

nothing to be happy about

I never thought I'd know the happiness of nothingness, like when we're both on the corner sofa and I'm in t-shirt and shorts with my headphones on watching videos on my phone, and you're wrapped in a duvet resting your feet on my lap, reading Maya Angelou by lamplight, and when one of us reaches out a hand the other takes it instinctively and we both make that sound you make when you know everything's going to be okay, and when one of us asks what the other wants from the takeaway he's already got an answer because he was moments away from asking the same thing.

acknowledgements

To my family, who have always supported me and my decisions, and always encouraged me and gave me the confidence to pursue writing and performing as valid ways to spend my time and effort.

To my partner, Vin, who has been my anchor, my shoulder to cry on, my light in the dark and my biggest cheerleader for more than the past decade with many more ahead of us. And, yes, some of these poems are about you but I promise only the nice ones.

To Carla, who encouraged me to process therapy easier by writing thoughts down as poems because we can finish something short instead of all those long projects we still both have hanging.

To Scarlett, the spark to my poetry powder keg. Your collection *Ache* let me know that it was okay to share my work with the world, work exploring content I previously thought no one would want to read. And when I reached out to tell you this you invited me along to workshops and gave me my first opportunities on the road to being a writer. You're a huge reason this collection even exists.

To Written Off for helping me get my words out into the world.

To NHS Mental Health Services, CBT therapy and antidepressants, the catalyst for this collection being a journey of reflection and self-improvement. Let's fund the NHS and remove medication stigma.

To my dad. You'll always be part of everything I pour my soul into. Particularly this collection. It's not your fault, it turns out I didn't handle trauma very well as a teenager so that one's on me. My bad.

notes

Some of the poems in this collection have notes on their origins:

The Sleeping Man was written when I was sixteen after the passing of my father. I considered editing or rewriting the piece for this collection but ultimately decided to keep it as written back in 2006.

Three Flies on the Severed Head of a Mouse appeared in Natter Bolton's Natterlogue #3.

The Cruel Face of Lazarus was published in vol. 3 of Swim Press.

Helicopter uses the format A Gram of &s, devised by Terrance Hayes.

Hometown Magnification first appeared in the pamphlet *The Words of Others are All We Have*, a conversational project co-written with Louise Machen and published by Hedgehog Press in April 2024.

Brid was published in Bent Key's *Ey Up Again* Anthology in Nov 2023.

The following poems first appeared on the Visual Verse website:
I Have No Body (vol. 8 – chapter 11)
Still (vol. 9 – chapter 10)
Broken Things Make for Gorgeous Sculptures (vol. 10 – chapter 10)

Soundtrack to a Life use lyrics from each song on the subtitled album:
A Certain Trigger – Maxïmo Park (2005)
High as Hope – Florence and the Machine (2018)
Wall of Arms – The Maccabees (2009)

about the author

J. Daniel West was born and raised in Hull, East Yorkshire, where he lived in the same house for eighteen years until he made the entirely rational decision to attend a university 300 miles away on the south coast. After a few years in London he returned to the north and settled in Manchester. He's always been a writer and turned to poetry when medication and therapy coincided with a global pandemic, and the shorter nature of the medium allowed him to process his weekly events. All the Rot became a diary of sorts, exploring how anxiety, grief and identity crises demand attention for the sake of self-improvement.

about the publisher

Written Off is a publishing company founded in and run from the North of England. It came into existence after Founder Rebecca Kenny's arrival home from hospital following a car crash in which she broke her neck, back, pelvis, sternum and sacrum. Its logo, an open umbrella, acts as a symbol of change, new starts, risk and taking a chance on the unknown.

Having her car written off, her career written off, and then being somewhat written off herself, Rebecca chose the company's name with an aim to reclaim power from adversity and show that just because society maintains a status quo, that doesn't mean you can't make waves.

Written Off do not charge for submissions, we do not charge to publish and we make space for writers who may struggle to access traditional publishing houses, specifically writers who are neuro-divergent or otherwise marginalised. We never ask anyone to write for free, and we like to champion authentic voices.

All of our beautiful covers are designed by independent queer artists. Please do take the time to follow their work.

Find us online at writtenoffpublishing.com